This book belongs to

Izabella.f

Copyright © 2012

# make believe ideas ltd

The Wilderness, Berkhamsted, Hertfordshire, HP4 2AZ, UK.
501 Nelson Place, P.O. Box 141000, Nashville, TN 37214-1000, USA.

www.makebelieveideas.com

Written by Tim Bugbird.
Illustrated by Lara Ede.
Designed by Annie Simpson and Sarah Vince.

# Izzy the Ice-cream Fairy

Tim Bugbird · Lara Ede

make believe ideas

Once upon a time,
in a **sunny**, sandy land,
lived **Izzy**, Mo, and Mia
at a pretty **ice-cream** stand.

The **fairy friends**
scooped ice cream
from their famous **ice-cream** well
to sell in **rainbow** flavors, in a crispy wafer shell.

And for a treat, their fairy wands sent showers, in all directions,

of candy jewels and chocolate chips, to top the iced confections.

They saved up every penny
to fund their carnival float

and every year, for Best in Show, they **won** the fairies' vote!

Then, early one summer,
they peered inside their well,
expecting flowing ice cream,
but there was nothing
left to sell!

The well had run
**completely** dry.
**Why?**
They had no clue.

But being **modern** fairies,
they **knew** just what to do!

Izzy surfed the **fairynet** for places **cold** and **chilly** with ice cream in **abundance**, but the results were just **too silly!**

If you said them **fast** enough, they sounded almost right, but two made Izzy **laugh** out loud, and one was just a **fright!**

"Where can I find **ice cream**?" Tap, tap, tap . . . .

EYES GREEN

"No, that's not right!"

MICE QUEEN

"No, that's not right!"

I SCREAM

"No!
That's definitely
not right!"

"Yes!"

Izzy finally found a place
with no palms, sea, or sand.
It was **far away** but perfect –
she'd discovered Ice-cream Land!

Izzy said, "That's funny,

our land is **warm** and **sunny**,

and since our ice-cream well ran dry,

we can't make any **money**."

"Can we work **together**? This feels like such good **luck**."
"Grab a **shovel**," said the Queen, "and I'll call

RENT-A-TRUCK!"

They dug and dug
and dug
and dug,
until it was quite clear,
their ice-cream haul
would be enough
to last at least a year!

ICE 1

The journey home
was **hampered** by fog
and **long**,
**dark** nights,

so Mo and Mia
lit their path
with lanterns and
fairy lights!

The trip took so **much longer**
than Izzy thought it would
and as they neared the **beach**, she cried,
"**Oh, no**, this isn't good!
The **carnival** starts today –
whatever will we ride?
It's way **too late** to make our float,
our hands are simply tied!"

But fortune had, for Izzy, one last big surprise:

all along the road ahead were floats of every size!

The fairies' truck joined the line, with its beautiful **glowing** lights.

It was just as good as a carnival float — a splendid, sparkling sight!

The fairies got to work,
serving ice cream to the crowd.
They made it home just in time
and had never felt so proud.

ice cream

Their float did not win Best in Show,
but Izzy didn't mind,
for the love and joy that filled the day
was a prize of a better kind!

Izzy, Mo, and Mia made the perfect fairy team, and now they knew just who to call when they needed more ice cream!